Angela Nicely

To Emily and Lucy ~ A M

For Nancy ~ D R

STRIPES PUBLISHING
An imprint of the Little Tiger Group
1 The Coda Centre, 189 Munster Road,
London SW6 6AW

A paperback original
First published in Great Britain in 2017

Text copyright © Alan MacDonald, 2017
Illustrations copyright © David Roberts, 2017

ISBN: 978-1-84715-777-5

The right of Alan MacDonald and David Roberts to
be identified as the author and illustrator of this work
respectively has been asserted by them in accordance
with the Copyright, Designs and Patents Act, 1988.

A CIP catalogue record for this book is available
from the British Library.

Printed and bound in the UK.

10 9 8 7 6 5 4 3 2 1

Angela Nicely

Starstruck!

ALAN MACDONALD ILLUSTRATED BY DAVID ROBERTS

stripes

Have you read the other
Angela Nicely books?

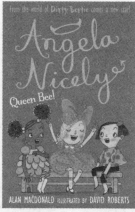

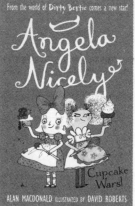

Contents

Chapter 1

Angela bounced into the kitchen.

"Mu-um," she said. "You know my favourite band in the whole wide world?"

"I think you may have mentioned them," said Mrs Nicely.

For weeks Angela had been talking about New Boyz – the best boy band in the world. Angela knew all their names: J.J., Nick, Jack and, most importantly, Zac, the lead singer. All her friends agreed that Zac was completely dreamy. Angela knew all the band's songs and drove her parents mad by singing them endlessly.

"Well," said Angela, "you won't believe it but they're coming to the Arena next Saturday. Isn't that amazing?"

"Amazing," said Mrs Nicely, clearing the table.

"So I was thinking…" began Angela.

"Out of the question," said Mrs Nicely. "You are NOT going to the concert."

Angela pouted. "Ohhh. Why not? Tiffany's going … and Laura and Maisie want to go."

"I'm sure they do," said Mrs Nicely. "But have their parents agreed?"

"Well, not yet," admitted Angela.

"You're far too young to be going to pop concerts," said her mum.

"But *you* could take me," Angela pleaded. "Tiffany's mum is taking her."

Mrs Nicely rolled her eyes. She couldn't think of anything worse. A concert with thousands of screaming girls. She'd have to listen to New Boyz and Angela singing in her ear all night. It would be unbearable. On the other hand, Mrs Charmers was taking Tiffany and she would probably go on about how fabulous it was for weeks.

"All right, I'll think about it," sighed Mrs Nicely. "But I'm not making any promises."

Angela clapped her hands. After all, what was there to think about?

Over supper that evening Angela returned to the subject.

"Dad, has Mum told you about the concert?"

"What concert?" said Dad.

"Next Saturday – New Boyz are coming to the Arena," Angela replied.

"Never heard of them. Are they famous?" asked Mr Nicely.

"Da-ad!" groaned Angela. "They're only the best band in the whole wide world! And Mum says she'll take me – maybe, probably."

Dad shrugged. "Well, if your mum wants to go it's fine with me," he said.

"Obviously I don't *want* to go but Angela is desperate," said Mrs Nicely. "And besides, Linda Charmers is taking Tiffany."

Dad raised his eyebrows.

"Oh, well, if Tiffany is going that settles it," he said.

"Will you take me, Mum?" begged Angela. "Pleeeease! And can Maisie and Laura come, too?"

Mrs Nicely groaned. "Yes, all right!" she said. "But only if their parents give their permission."

Angela whooped. She couldn't wait to ring her friends to tell them the great news. They were actually going to see New Boyz in concert. It was going to be the best night of her life!

Chapter 2

At school the next day the girls couldn't talk about anything else.

"I can't believe that we're actually going!" sighed Angela.

"Nor me," said Laura. "It's like a dream come true."

"Do you think we'll see Zac?" asked Maisie.

"Of course we'll see Zac," said Angela. "He's the lead singer."

At that moment Tiffany Charmers skipped by.

"Oh Tiffany, you'll never guess what," cried Angela. "We're going to see New Boyz!"

"You are not!" scoffed Tiffany.

"We are!" said Maisie. "Angela's mum's taking us."

Tiffany stuck her nose in the air. "Well anyway, I bet you haven't got good tickets," she said. "You're probably sitting miles from the stage."

"Why, where are you sitting?" asked Angela.

"Right at the front," boasted Tiffany. "The tickets were *ever* so expensive but Mummy didn't mind. She says I deserve the best!"

Angela pulled a face. Trust snooty Tiffany to have the best seats in the house. She always had to go one better than everyone else.

"We don't care where we're sitting," said Maisie.

"No, as long as we're going," agreed Laura.

"Fine," trilled Tiffany. "But I'll be so

close I'll probably be able to touch Zac's hand!"

This was too much. Angela glared. "So what?" she said. "I'm actually going to meet him. So there!"

Everyone turned to look at her open-mouthed.

"ANG-ER-LA, you big liar!" cried Tiffany.

"It's true," claimed Angela. "My dad knows someone who is friends with New Boyz and he can fix it for me to meet Zac."

"I don't believe you!" sneered Tiffany.

"Don't then," said Angela.

Tiffany folded her arms. "You're really actually going to meet Zac?"

Angela nodded. "That's what I said."

"Okay, I want to see a picture of you and Zac together, then I might believe you," said Tiffany.

Just then the bell rang for the start of school.

"Are you serious?" Laura whispered as they lined up. "Who's this person who's friends with Zac?"

"There isn't one," said Maisie. "Angela made it up, as usual."

"Only because Tiffany made me," huffed Angela. "She's such a big show off!"

"Yes, but what are you going to do?" asked Laura. "Tiffany wants to see a picture!"

Angela frowned. "You never know, I might meet Zac," she said. "He's going to be there, isn't he?"

"Angela, thousands of people will be there," said Laura.

"And Zac will be on stage – you're never going to meet him," said Maisie.

Angela sighed. Why couldn't she keep her big mouth shut? She should never have told Tiffany such a whopping great lie. If she didn't get a picture of herself with Zac, Tiffany would make sure the story was all round the school.

Chapter 3

On Saturday night Angela and her friends joined the crowds flooding into the Arena. Angela looked around excitedly. She'd never seen so many people.

"Now, a few rules before it starts," said Mrs Nicely. "We keep together, stay in our seats and please, please, no screaming."

"What about when they come on stage?" asked Angela.

"Especially when they come on stage," said Mrs Nicely.

They went to find their seats. It turned out that they were in row ZZ, about a million miles from the stage. The only way they were going to see the band was by watching the giant screen. Angela frowned – she'd been secretly hoping she might somehow bump into Zac but now she realized she'd have to climb over two thousand people to even get near him. Tiffany was going to be so smug when she saw her at school on Monday.

The house lights suddenly went down, plunging them into darkness.

Laura squealed.

"*Please*, no screaming," warned Mrs Nicely.

Suddenly New Boyz appeared on the stage, bathed in spotlights.

"AAAAAAAARGH!" screamed the girls.

At the interval, Angela and her friends went to the toilet while Mrs Nicely queued for drinks. "That was incredible!" said Angela, as she washed her hands.

"I've nearly lost my voice," said Maisie.

"Oh, hello Ang-er-la!" trilled Tiffany, spotting her. "How are your seats?"

"Er ... great," said Angela. "We can see everything."

"We're so close, it's amazing," said Tiffany. "Zac actually waved at me!"

"Really?" said Angela. "I think he waves at everyone."

"Anyway, you're actually going to meet him," said Tiffany. "When's the big moment?"

"Oh soon, after the concert," lied Angela, turning red.

"*Amazing!*" cried Tiffany. "Say hello from me and don't forget that picture – otherwise I might think you're telling a big fat lie. Bye, Ang-er-la!" She dried her hands and danced off.

Angela's shoulders drooped. Seeing Tiffany had spoilt the whole evening. How was she meant to get a picture of her and Zac? Their seats were miles away from the stage and right now he was probably in his dressing room. *Wait a minute*, thought Angela, *his dressing room…*

It had to be somewhere in the building!
She followed Maisie and Laura out of
the toilets.

"Quick this way," she whispered.
"We don't have much time!"

"Where are we going?" asked Laura.

"To find Zac's dressing room of
course," answered Angela.

"ANGELA, you are bonkers!" said
Maisie.

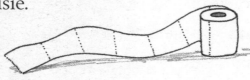

They hurried along the corridor
through crowds of fans. At last they
came to some double doors with a sign
saying "NO ENTRY!" A giant of a man
wearing dark glasses guarded the door.

"Let's go back," whispered Laura. But
Angela stepped forwards.

"Excuse me," she said. "I'm a friend of Zac's."

The bouncer looked her up and down. "Is that right?" he growled.

"Yes, can I go and see him? I promised I would," said Angela, which was sort of true.

"Sure," said the giant. "Just show me your backstage pass."

Angela's face fell. "Oh, um … I think I must have lost it," she said.

The giant shook his head. "Sorry, missy, no pass, no entry. That's the rules."

Angela returned to her friends. It was hopeless. She would never get to meet Zac.

"Never mind, let's get back," said Laura. "Your mum will be going mad."

"And we'll miss the second half," said Maisie.

They started to hurry back the way they'd come. They hadn't gone far when a woman passed them dragging a clothes rail with four suits on coat hangers. Angela stared. They could only be heading for one place – the band's dressing room. This was her chance. She doubled back following the clothes rail and ducked behind it.

It was a few seconds before her friends realized she'd gone. Maisie looked round and caught sight of Angela's shoes perched on the rail beneath the suits.

"ANGELA!" she hissed. "WHAT ARE YOU DOING?"

A hand stuck out from the suits and gave her a thumbs up. Maisie groaned. Sometimes Angela was unbelievable.

Chapter 4

The clothes rail trundled on for what seemed an age. At last it halted. Angela heard a loud knock on a door. A voice answered and the clothes rail was pulled into a room.

"Oh thanks, leave it there," said a voice.

The door slammed shut.

The room was small and brightly lit.
Cautiously Angela peeped out from
between the suits. It was them – New
Boyz! She was actually in the same
room, breathing the same air! JJ, Nick
and Jack lolled on chairs, sipping water
and checking their phones. Zac was
combing his glossy brown hair in the
mirror.

Angela's heart thumped. She hadn't
planned what to do next. Should she
jump out and surprise them? What if
they called the giant guard she'd met
earlier? Or the police? Even worse,
what if they called her mum?

Zac looked at his watch. "Five
minutes, boys," he said. "Better get
ready."

Angela clapped a hand over her

mouth. The suits! Any moment now they'd take them off the rail and discover her! She raised herself to look out but the clothes rail was starting to tip. Help! She was falling…

CRASH!

Angela landed on the floor in a tangled heap of suits and coat hangers. The band jumped up in surprise.

"Where did YOU come from?" asked Zac.

Angela struggled to her feet. "I was hiding," she said. "I just ... um ... wanted to meet you. I'm Angela."

"Quite an entrance, Angela," grinned Zac.

"You can't stay here," frowned Nick. "We're on stage in a minute."

A knock on the door made Angela jump.

"Last call!" said a voice.

"Please don't tell!" begged Angela. "I didn't mean any harm. It's just I told Tiffany I was going to meet you but I made it up, so I had to find a way to get in ... and ... and..."

She trailed off, hanging her head. Suddenly she realized this was all a big mistake. She should never have hidden among the suits, or worse, gone off without telling her mum. Now she was in big trouble with everyone.

"So who's this Tiffany then?" said Zac.

"She's in my class and she's sitting in the front row," said Angela. "She's such a show-off smarty-pants."

"A show-off smarty-pants?" said Zac. "They're the worst. Did you come with her?"

Angela shook her head. "No, I'm with my friends and my mum. She's going to kill me!"

"Don't worry," said Zac. "I've got an idea. Why don't we give smarty-pants Tiffany a surprise?"

He put on his jacket and opened the door. "Are you coming?" he asked.

Back in the Arena, Mrs Nicely was getting worried. Where on earth was Angela? Laura and Maisie had returned with some story that they'd left Angela queuing for popcorn.

"What's she *doing*?" demanded Mrs Nicely. "I'm going to find her."

"No! She's coming," said Maisie.

"Once she's got an ice cream," added Laura.

Mrs Nicely frowned. "I thought you said popcorn," she cried. "I want the truth, Laura – where is she?"

Laura bit her lip. "She's gone to see Zac," she mumbled.

"ZAC!" yelled Mrs Nicely, jumping up. "You mean Zac in the band?"

Just then the lights went down and screams greeted the band back on stage. Mrs Nicely looked up. She counted five figures on the giant screen. The fifth one wasn't a member of the band, though. It was a small girl with blond hair and a huge grin on her face.

"ANGELA!" gasped Mrs Nicely, clutching her seat.

"Welcome back!" said Zac. "Say hello to the newest member of the band – Angela."

Angela twirled and took a bow.

"This next one's for Tiffany who thought Angela was making it up," said Zac. "Hi, Tiffany!"

In the front row, Angela spotted Tiffany with her mouth hanging open. She gave her a big wave.

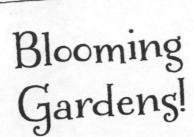

Blooming Gardens!

Chapter 1

Angela ran out into the garden. She was playing Hide and Seek with Laura and Maisie but where could she hide? Her eyes fell on her mum's new pond. It was backed by long reedy grass, perfect for hiding. She hurried towards it.

"ANGELA!"

Uh oh. She hadn't noticed her mum

weeding in the flowerbeds.

"Keep away from that pond," warned Mrs Nicely sternly. "I've told you before."

"But Mum, I've got to hide!" begged Angela.

"Not in the garden," said Mrs Nicely.

Angela blinked. "Why not?" she said.

"Because tomorrow is the Best Kept Garden Competition and people will be coming to look round," explained Mrs Nicely. "I've just finished weeding the garden and the last thing I need is you trampling on the flower beds."

"I won't," promised Angela. "But I've got to hide somewhere."

"Hide indoors," said Mrs Nicely.

"MUUUM! There's no time!" groaned Angela, throwing up her hands.

It was too late – she heard the back door open and Laura's footsteps getting closer. Angela dived behind the garden bench.

"I can see you, Angela!" sang Laura, from the top of the steps.

Angela's head peeped into view.

"It's not fair, I wasn't ready!" she grumbled.

"I counted to ten," said Laura. "I found Maisie, too."

Maisie came outside to join them.

"I'm tired of Hide and Seek," she said. "Let's play something else."

"We can't play in the garden because we're not allowed to touch anything," said Angela, rolling her eyes.

"I'm sorry, girls, but I've entered the Best Kept Garden Competition," Mrs Nicely explained. "I'm really hoping I might win this year."

"Wowee!" said Laura.

"Of course I'll have to beat Mrs Nettles, she always wins," sighed Mrs Nicely. "Last year I stood a really good chance until an army of slugs invaded my primroses."

"Slugs? Eww!" said Maisie, pulling a face.

"Yes, they eat the plants," said Mrs Nicely. "I wouldn't be surprised if Mrs Nettles had something to do with it. That woman would stop at nothing to win."

Angela's eyes grew bigger. She'd never met Mrs Nettles but she sounded really mean. Perhaps she'd crept into their garden leading an army of slugs? Who knew that gardeners could be so sneaky just to win a competition?

"Anyway, I have my ornamental pond this year," said Mrs Nicely. "That's my trump card to impress the judge."

"Is there a prize if you win?" asked Angela.

"I don't care about prizes, I take part for the pleasure of showing my garden," said her mum. "Although I think the winner gets a gift voucher for seventy-five pounds."

Seventy-five pounds – just for growing flowers! thought Angela. Think what you could do with all that money! For months Angela had been begging her parents to buy a trampoline for the garden. Her mum said they were too expensive but surely with the prize money they could afford one?

That settles it, decided Angela. *We have to beat mean old Mrs Nettles and win the competition.*

Chapter 2

Later Angela and her friends sat on the garden bench drinking lemonade. It was too hot to go inside and anyway they had things to discuss.

"It is a nice garden," said Laura.

"Yes, but is it good enough to win the competition?" asked Angela.

"I don't know," said Maisie, looking

around. "It's nice but it's not really special, is it?"

Angela frowned. "It's got a pond, that's Mum's trump card," she said.

"Yes, but there isn't much to do," argued Maisie. "I mean you can smell the flowers but that's boring. What it needs is a tree house or something."

Laura nodded. "Yes, a tree house or maybe a chocolate fountain."

"And a trampoline," added Angela. "If we win the competition, we'll get a trampoline."

"Really?" said Laura.

"Definitely," said Angela. "We'll have seventy-five pounds to spend, so what else would we do with it?"

She closed her eyes trying to imagine the garden with a trampoline on the

lawn. It would be great for bouncing
up and down so she could spy on what
Bertie was up to next door.

Angela sighed. "You're right, if we're going to win it needs more than just flowers and a smelly old pond."

"You should get some gnomes," suggested Laura.

"Gnomes?" said Angela.

"Yes, garden gnomes. My gran has lots of them," said Laura. "They're funny little men who sit on toadstools, push wheelbarrows and go fishing. They'd make the garden more fun."

Angela had never seen a garden gnome before but they sounded like a good idea. She jumped to her feet.

"I know!" she said. "There's lots of stuff we could use in my bedroom."

"What stuff?" asked Maisie.

"I'll show you," said Angela. "Come on!"

Half an hour later Angela found her
mum in the kitchen, baking for the
next day.

"Come and look what we've done!"
Angela cried, beaming.

Mrs Nicely frowned. "Done? Where?"
she said.

"In the garden," replied Angela.

Mrs Nicely turned pale. In the
garden? *Her* garden – the day before
the competition? Oh no! Whenever
Angela did something helpful it always
ended in disaster.

Mrs Nicely hurried outside and
looked around. Thankfully the
greenhouse was still standing and none
of the flowers had been dug up.

"What am I looking at?" she asked.

"The garden!" replied Angela. "Can't you see? We didn't have any gnomes so we used my toys!"

Mrs Nicely stepped down on to the lawn. Laura and Maisie were waiting excitedly. Mrs Nicely gasped as she caught sight of a monkey hanging upside down from the cherry tree. By the pond a teddy bear and a yellow duck were dabbling their feet in the water. There was a doll's tea party in full swing under the azaleas. Everywhere she looked soft toy puppies, kittens and blue elephants peeped from bushes or flower beds.

"Well?" said Angela. "What do you think? It's much more fun, isn't it?"

Mrs Nicely silently counted to five.

"Take them away, Angela," she said. "Right now."

"What, ALL of them?" cried Angela.

"All of them," said Mrs Nicely. "And please, please, don't do anything else to my garden or I may scream."

The three girls watched her march back to the house. Angela sighed. The trouble with parents was they were no fun at all, she thought.

Chapter 3

On Saturday morning Mrs Nicely
was up early, watering the plants and
inspecting her garden for dandelions
and slugs. Angela and her friends had
begged to help so she'd put them in
charge of refreshments. They couldn't
do any harm serving cakes and drinks –
at least that's what she told herself.

At eleven o'clock visitors started to arrive. Angela was amazed that so many people wanted to look round their boring garden. She sat at the refreshments table with Maisie and Laura, trying not to eat all the cakes. Her mum stood greeting people as they arrived.

"Keep an eye out for Mrs Shrub, she's the judge," she explained.

"How will we know her?" asked Angela.

"She has grey hair and glasses on a cord round her neck," said Mrs Nicely. "You can't miss her."

"Shall we give her cake?" asked Laura.

"Of course – tea, cake, biscuits,

anything she wants," replied Mrs
Nicely. "Just be sure to make a good
impression."

Angela nodded. Winning the
competition – and getting a trampoline
– depended on impressing Mrs Shrub.

"Oh, and I nearly forgot," said Mrs
Nicely. "I wouldn't be surprised if Mrs
Nettles drops in to spy on my garden."

"The slug lady?" said Angela.

Her mum nodded. "She's thin as a
sparrow. Look out for anyone who's
acting oddly."

"Oddly?" said Laura.

"Yes, picking flowers or treading on
plants," said Mrs Nicely. "I don't trust
that woman, she'll do anything to win."

Angela frowned. There was a lot to
remember. It would be so much easier

if everyone wore name badges.

All that morning they were busy serving refreshments. Angela kept a close eye on the visitors, trying to spot the judge. At last she found her.

"That's HER! Mrs Shrub!" hissed Angela. "By the fence."

The others looked over. An old lady was smelling the roses. She had bushy grey hair and a pair of glasses dangling from a cord round her neck.

"Are you sure it's her?" said Laura.

"Of course it's her," replied Angela. "She's exactly as Mum said. I'll bring her over."

Soon the old lady was sat in a chair while they waited on her like the Queen.

"Have some more cake," said Maisie.

"Well thank you, dear."

"Would you like another cup of tea?" asked Laura.

"If it's no trouble," smiled the old lady.

"So, what do you think of our garden?" asked Angela, getting to the point.

"Oh, it's a treat," said the old lady. "So neat and tidy and I love the little pond."

"Is it the best garden you've seen today?" asked Angela.

"Easily!" said the old lady. "Mind you, I've only been to two."

Angela looked pleased. Mrs Shrub had lots more gardens to inspect but if she kept eating cake she might not get round to all of them.

Chapter 4

The visitors kept coming all morning.
Angela had to run to the kitchen to
fetch more cakes. When she returned
the old lady had dozed off. Her mouth
was open and she still had a half-eaten
lemon slice on her plate. Angela
wondered if they ought to wake her
up. It was difficult to judge gardens

with your eyes closed. Laura grabbed
Angela's arm.

"You know the mean slug lady?"
she hissed. "I think she's here!"

"Where?" gasped Angela.

"There!" said Laura. She
pointed to a woman near
the greenhouse, inspecting
the fruit bushes. Angela
tried to remember what
her mum had said –
"thin as a sparrow".
This woman *was* thin
with her hair scraped
back in a bun.

"She ate a
raspberry!"
whispered
Laura.

"Yes, we saw her do it!" said Maisie.

"And she keeps touching all the flowers," said Laura.

Angela nodded, it was definitely Mrs Nettles. What a nerve – sneaking into their garden and stealing their raspberries! Angela saw she had a large black handbag over her arm.

"I bet she's got all the slugs in there!" she whispered.

"YUCK!" said Maisie.

"That's how she sneaks them in," said Angela. "Don't you remember the slugs ate all our flowers last year?"

"Shouldn't we tell your mum?" asked Laura anxiously.

Angela glanced over. Her mum was busy chatting to a thin woman with her back to them. Angela knew better than to interrupt but if they waited it might be too late. Something had to be done before Mrs Nettles spoiled their chances of winning the competition.

"Leave this to me," said Angela.

"What are you going to do?" asked Maisie.

"You'll see," said Angela. "She won't come round here again with her smelly bag of slugs!"

"Hello, I'm Angela!" said Angela, smiling sweetly at the woman. "It's my mum's garden."

The visitor looked at her. "Hello," she said.

"Would you like to see our fish?" asked Angela.

"You have fish?" asked the woman.

"Yes, two – Tiffany and Bertie," said Angela, making it up on the spot.

She led the way down the garden to the ornamental pond.

"I don't see any fish," said the woman.

"I expect they're hiding in the lilies. They're a bit shy," said Angela. "You have to look really hard."

The woman leaned forwards over the pond. Angela glanced round. It was now or never. She stared at Mrs Nettles' black handbag, imagining the slimy slugs squirming inside. That did it. She reached out and gave the woman a shove in the back.

The woman wobbled on one leg, then toppled forwards…

Angela Nicely

"Oh... OHHHHH...!"

KERSPLASH!

"AAAAAARGH!"

Everyone heard the scream and came running. They found a woman sitting in the pond, fully clothed and dripping wet.

"She… She pushed me!" squawked the woman, pointing at Angela.

"ANGELA! YOU DIDN'T?" cried Mrs Nicely.

"Not on purpose," said Angela. "Anyway, she's got slugs in her bag."

"Slugs? Are you mad?" said the woman.

"And she's been eating our raspberries!" said Angela.

"I ate one!" cried the woman. "It's the judge's job to sample the fruit."

"The judge's?" said Angela.

"This is Mrs Shrub – who is judging the competition," said Mrs Nicely, holding her head in her hands.

Angela blinked. "Mrs Shrub? But we thought *she* was the judge."

She pointed at the little old lady who seemed to have woken up.

"Me? Oh, no, I'm not anyone, dear," said the old lady.

"But you're wearing your glasses on a string," said Angela.

"Like these you mean?" said the real Mrs Shrub, fishing a pair of glasses on a cord from her handbag.

Angela groaned. She'd pushed the wrong woman in the pond.

Mrs Shrub squelched out. Her dress clung wetly to her and there was green weed in her hair.

"Sorry," mumbled Angela. "Anyone can make a mistake. I thought you were mean Mrs Nettles."

"I AM NASTY MRS NETTLES,"
boomed a voice.

Angela turned. It was the thin woman
her mum had been talking to, and she
looked very cross. In fact everyone
looked a bit cross, especially her mum.

"Why didn't you tell me which one was the judge?" moaned Angela.

"I was busy!" snapped Mrs Nicely. "How *could* you, Angela? Go and fetch Mrs Shrub a towel."

Angela hurried off to the house. She wondered if now was a good time to ask her mum for a trampoline… Maybe not. Although that pond was going to have to go – it was nothing but trouble!

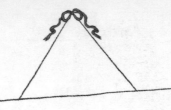

Problems, Problems!

Chapter 1

Angela found her mum reading a magazine at the kitchen table.

"Who's 'Dear Dora'?" asked Angela, looking over her shoulder.

"She's someone who helps people with their problems," said her mum.

"You mean like maths problems?" asked Angela.

"No, everyday problems. People write in and Dora gives them advice," said Mrs Nicely. "She's called an Agony Aunt."

Angela had never heard of an Agony Aunt but it sounded interesting.

"Can you read it out?" she asked.

Her mum groaned. "No! They're just problems about money or boyfriends or mothers who never get a moment's peace. Shouldn't you be getting ready for school?"

"I am," said Angela. "Could I do it?"

"Do what?"

"Be the Aunt in your magazine," said Angela. "I'm good at advice."

"I'm sure you are but you're far too young," said her mum.

"What if I was nine?" asked Angela.

Mrs Nicely shook her head. "You don't

have enough experience. Maybe when you're a lot older," she said. "Now where are your shoes?"

Angela went off to look for them. The more she thought about it, being an Agony Aunt seemed like the perfect job for her. For one thing she liked knowing other people's problems and also she knew lots of good advice. Rather than writing to "Dear Dora" people could send their problems to Auntie Angela…

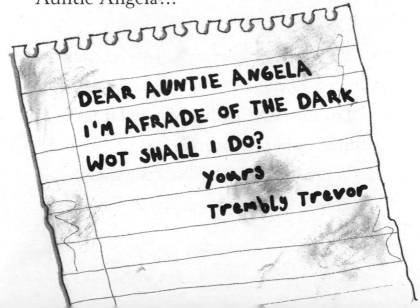

DEAR AUNTIE ANGELA
I'M AFRADE OF THE DARK
WOT SHALL I DO?
Yours
Trembly Trevor

Dear Trevor
KEEP THE LITE ON
    Love
        Auntie Angela

Angela found her shoes and quickly slipped them on. She decided she would definitely be an Agony Aunt when she was older. And in the meantime she could get some practice by sorting out her friends' problems.

On the way to school Angela made a start.

"So anyway, what are your problems?" she asked her friends.

Maisie looked puzzled. "What are you on about?" she said.

"Problems – everybody has problems," said Angela. "When I'm older I'm going to be an Agony Aunt in a magazine and help people with their problems, so I need to start practising now."

"Well, I can't think of any problems," said Maisie.

"Nor can I," said Laura.

"There must be something! Think!" cried Angela.

Laura frowned. "Well, there's my hair I suppose," she said.

"What about it?" asked Angela.

"I wish it was curlier like Maisie's," replied Laura.

Angela rolled her eyes. She doubted if "Dear Dora" wrote about people who wanted curlier hair. She would have to ask her classmates. There was bound to be someone with a really interesting problem that needed her advice.

Chapter 2

At school Angela went round the playground asking her classmates to explain their problems. The list she collected wasn't very exciting. Amanda Thribb had a tickly cough, Kelly had a hole in her sock and Sean had forgotten to bring his PE kit to school. None of these were the kind of problems needing Angela's advice.

"Maybe teachers have better problems," she said to Laura.

But as they reached the classroom, Laura found a note on their desk.

"It's for you, Angela," she said, handing it over.

The note had neat, tiny writing. Angela read it eagerly.

Dear Angela
I hurd you was asking for peeples problems. Well I have a BIG one.
No one seems to notice me.
I havent reely got any friends and I dont no what I can do about it.
PLEESE, PLEESE HELP!!!!!!!!

At last! thought Angela, someone who really needed her advice! But there was no name on the note. Who was it from?

"Did you see who left this?" she asked Laura.

Laura shook her head.

"But how am I supposed to help if I don't know who they are?" moaned Angela, throwing up her hands.

It was a mystery. Who did they know who felt forgotten and didn't have any friends? Angela looked around the class.

"Tiffany!" she cried. "Maybe she sent the note?"

"Tiffany Charmers?" laughed Maisie. "Everyone pays *her* attention. She's such a big show off!"

"And anyway she's got lots of friends," Laura pointed out.

"Not real friends," argued Angela. "They're just people she bosses about. I'm going to ask her."

She marched over to Tiffany's desk.

"Tiffany, I got your note!" whispered Angela. "You know, about your BIG PROBLEM."

Tiffany stared at her. "WHAT?" she said.

"You know… How no one pays you any attention and you don't have any friends," said Angela.

Tiffany looked annoyed. "Cheek! I've got millions of friends!" she said.

"Then why did you send me the note?" asked Angela.

"What note? You're raving potty, Angela!" said Tiffany. "Go and bother someone else!"

Just then Miss Darling came in.

"Angela Nicely!" she cried "Why are you out of your seat?"

Angela hurried back to her place. Perhaps Tiffany hadn't sent the note after all, she thought. As she sat down Angela noticed a dark haired girl staring at her. She pointed to herself then to Angela.

"Who's that?" Angela asked her friends.

Laura looked round. "That's Molly, she's the new girl," she replied.

Of course! thought Angela. *It must have been Molly who'd written the note!* Molly had started at their school a few weeks ago but she'd barely spoken three words since her first day. In fact, Angela had completely forgotten she existed! No wonder Molly needed help – and luckily for her she'd come to the right person. Auntie Angela was going to solve all her problems.

At morning break Angela brought Molly over to meet her friends.

"This is Molly," said Angela. "Nobody talks to her – which I think is terrible."

"*You* never talk to her," Maisie replied.

"Only because I've been busy," said Angela. "So anyway, she needs advice."

Molly shrugged helplessly. "I just don't really know anyone," she sighed.

They all tried to think of some good advice.

"I know, you could throw a party," said Maisie. "If you invite the whole class it'll make you really popular!"

"I don't think my mum would let me," said Molly.

"No," said Angela. "Anyway first you

need to get yourself noticed. You should talk more in class. It's no good sitting there quiet as a caterpillar."

"No," agreed Laura. "When we have News Time you should put up your hand."

"And say something interesting," added Maisie.

Molly looked doubtful. "What would I say?" she asked.

"Anything!" said Angela. "Just make it up – Tiffany does it all the time!"

After lunch they gathered on the carpet for News Time. Molly looked around nervously. Angela sat next to her in case she needed prompting.

"Right, who's got any news this week?"

asked Miss Darling.

Angela's hand shot up. "Molly has!" she cried.

"Lovely, Molly, and what's your news then?" asked Miss Darling.

Molly turned bright red. She stared at the carpet.

"Um… I might go swimming," she mumbled.

"How nice! And who's going swimming with you?" asked Miss Darling.

Molly blushed even deeper. "I … I don't know yet," she stammered.

"Well … I hope you have fun," smiled

Miss Darling. "So who else has got some news? Tiffany!"

Angela groaned. That hadn't worked at all! No one had shown the slightest interest in Molly's news. She should have said she was swimming with dolphins – that would have got everyone's attention! Besides, how was Molly going to get people's attention if she mumbled all the time? Angela never mumbled – in fact teachers often asked her to keep her voice down.

They were obviously going to have
to think again. Maybe Molly could
come top of the class, thought Angela.
But that wouldn't work because
Tiffany Charmers always came top at
everything. Angela frowned. Suddenly
an idea came to her. What if Molly
did something daring, something that
everyone would talk about for weeks?
That would get her noticed! But what?

Angela waited till they were back in
their seats. "I've got it," she whispered.
"Molly's got to do something really
daring."

"You mean like eating a worm?" asked
Laura.

"No, that'll just make her sick. I mean
something like playing a trick on
someone," said Angela.

"What about Tiffany?" said Maisie. "Or a teacher?"

"Yes, a teacher!" said Angela. "But not Miss Darling, it ought to be the meanest, scariest teacher in the school."

Maisie and Laura stared. "You don't mean … MISS BOOT?" they gasped.

Angela nodded. Miss Boot was the obvious choice. No one ever dared to play a trick on her. If Molly succeeded she would be a legend throughout the school.

MISS BOOT

Chapter 3

At first Molly thought they were joking. "You want me to play a trick on *Miss Boot?*" she said.

Angela nodded. "You wanted my advice – this is it," she said.

"But how will it help me make friends?" asked Molly.

"Because it's really daring," said Angela.

"Everyone will say, 'Look, there's Molly, the girl who played a trick on Miss Boot.'"

"I wouldn't do it, I'd be terrified," said Laura.

"Then why have I got to do it?" asked Molly.

"Because it will work," argued Angela. "Once everyone's talking about you they'll all want to be your friend. You'll see."

Molly wasn't so sure. Besides she'd seen Miss Boot in assembly and she looked like a fire-breathing dragon.

"But I'll get into trouble," she moaned.

"Only if you get caught," said Angela. "All you have to do is sneak up and stick a sign on her back."

"What sort of sign?" asked Molly.

Angela had written two words on a piece of card. The others burst out laughing when they saw it.

"I CAN'T DO THAT!" moaned Molly. "What if she sees it?"

"She won't," said Angela. "But everyone else will and that's the joke."

Molly shook her head. "Couldn't you do it?" she begged.

"There's no point in ME doing it!" said Angela. "I've already got hundreds of friends!"

At lunchtime they all trooped outside. Miss Boot was on playground duty with Mr Weakly.

"Now's your chance," said Angela. "Sneak over while she's busy chatting."

Molly reluctantly took the sign. "I don't think I can," she whimpered.

"Of course you can," said Angela. "We'll be right here watching you."

Molly took a deep breath. She circled round the playground until she was behind the teachers. No one paid her any attention. Molly looked back at Angela, who gave her a thumbs up.

"You just have to show who's in charge," Miss Boot was saying.

"I do try," sighed Mr Weakly. "I've been practising my angry face in the mirror."

Angela watched, holding her breath as Molly crept closer. If Miss Boot turned round now, Molly was in deep doo-doo. Molly reached out a trembling hand and stuck the sign on Miss Boot's back.

"Please DON'T do that!" snapped Miss Boot.

"Do what?" asked Mr Weakly, blinking.

"Tap me on the back – it's very annoying," said Miss Boot.

"But I didn't!" bleated Mr Weakly.

"Well, someone did, I felt it," said Miss Boot. She turned round but there was no one to be seen.

Chapter 4

"I did it!" panted Molly, racing back. "I don't think she saw me."

"Well done, Molly," said Angela. "Now we wait for the fun to start."

Soon after the bell rang for the end of lunch break.

"LINE UP! NO TALKING!" barked Miss Boot.

Molly and Angela joined the line with everyone else. Miss Boot faced them with her arms folded. Angela wished she would turn round so that everyone could see the sign on her back.

"SILENCE! I SAID NO TALKING!" boomed Miss Boot.

Mr Weakly was gaping at her like a short-sighted fish. He seemed to be trying to say something.

"What's the matter with you?" demanded Miss Boot. "Are you sick?"

Mr Weakly shook his head. He dropped his voice.

"Ah … um … Miss Boot," he said. "There's, er, something on your back."

"ON MY BACK?" repeated Miss Boot. "What are you babbling about?"

She spun round revealing Angela's sign stuck to her back.

A wave of giggling broke out among the children.

"STOP THAT AT ONCE!" barked Miss Boot. "What's so funny?"

She twisted round and round, trying to see what was on her back. The giggling grew louder. Angela, Laura and

Maisie were almost helpless. In the end
Mr Weakly put an end to the joke by
removing the sign and handing it to
Miss Boot. Her eyes
bulged. She shook
with rage.

"WHO…
DID…
THIS?" she
thundered.

There was
a long silence.
Angela's hand
waved in the air.

"Please,
Miss Boot, it
was Molly,"
she said
proudly.

"ANGELA!" hissed Laura.

"What?" said Angela. What was the use of Molly's daring act if she didn't take the credit for it?

"Molly Johnson!" barked Miss Boot. "Come here!"

Molly glared at Angela and trailed out to the front.

"I am surprised at you, Molly," said Miss Boot. "Perhaps you think this kind of thing is funny? Did you write this?"

Molly shook her head.

"Then who did?"

"Angela," said Molly truthfully.

Angela sunk her head in her hands.

"Ah, now we're getting somewhere," said Miss Boot grimly. "Angela Nicely, come here! You can both go and stand outside the Head's office.

I'm sure she'll be *very* interested to hear your explanation."

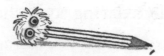

Five minutes later Angela and Molly stood outside Miss Skinner's office. Their classmates filed past on the way to class.

"You're bonkers, Molly!" said Amanda Thribb in awe.

"I thought she was going to kill you!" said Kelly.

"It was funny, though," grinned Sean.

"You see?" said Angela, when they'd gone. "I told you it would work – everyone's talking about you."

Molly smiled shyly but just then the office door swung open and Miss Skinner appeared.

"Right, inside, both of you," she snapped.

They crept in.

"What do we say?" whispered Molly.

Angela gulped. She knew lots of good advice but, right now, nothing that would save them.